THIS TIME OF YEAR

Written by Joseph Petrucelli
Illustrated by Mahmoud Mohammadi

Petronia Tone daydreams as she gazes out her window. The window sill is completely covered with snow and icicles from that day's big snow storm.

Fortunately for Petronia, the snowstorm canceled school and she now has more time to practice her song.

It doesn't take long before Petronia becomes bored practicing. She lays her head down on the windowsill and dozes off, dreaming of singing on a big stage.

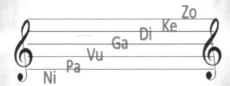

The window now open, the chant, "Practice. Practice. Practice," is louder than ever. Within seconds, Petronia finds herself joining in with the beam of light. These are the same notes her dad tells her to practice all the time.

WAIT, I GOT IT! I'LL JUST "WISHETTE" ON ALL THESE DANDELIONS LIKE MY MOM SAYS AND I WON'T NEED TO PRACTICE.

As all the dandelion "Wishettes" continue to fly past, Petronia wishes to sing great in front of her family. Her wish puts a big smile on her face, thinking her practice problem is solved.

Suddenly the music, loud chanting voice, dandelions, and beam of light are gone, replaced by laughter. Petronia looks at the street below.

Petronia can hear all the laughter coming from her
friends Lars, Boomer, and others, shouting, "No school!"
while watching Sunny make a snowbird-angel in the snow.

The laughter grows louder and louder. Even her teacher
Ms. Angela and other neighbors join in all the fun.

Because of all the laughter, no one hears Petronia.

Now excited, Petronia hops out her window onto the ledge. Just as she gets ready to take off, that same voice and music echo loudly, "You haven't finished practicing your song!"

Startled by the loud voice and music, Petronia looks up. The same bright light blinds her, causing her to slip off the ledge!

Petronia gathers herself quickly, and flies toward her friends. Unfortunately, Petronia doesn't realize how fast she's flying and how close she is to the snow pile.

None of her friends were sure what was flying toward them!

Petronia hits the snow pile with a loud thud. Ms. Angela, the only one who realizes it's Petronia, looks on in disbelief.

Petronia's Uncle Miles, dad, and mom all call out from their apartment window above.

Petronia snaps out of her daze.

Sunny is concerned about his friend. "Are you okay?" he asks.

"I didn't practice enough," she says. "I have to sing my song for my family, and my dad already knows I am not ready."

With that, Petronia trudges off through the snow.

I SHOULD HAVE PRACTICED.

Nervous, Petronia bites her nails as she walks up the stairs to her apartment.

Out of breath, Petronia opens the door.

"Hi, everyone, I am here to perform my new song, called 'This Time of Year!' Here it goes! A one-and-a-two..." She sings, but she's way off key.

Her dad yells, "You're mumbling the words, Petronia. Didn't you practice?"

Her performance is a total disaster. All her Wishetting on all those dandelions didn't work.

Petronia feels dejected when suddenly there's a knock on the door.

"Hang on, hang on, everybody, one second," her dad Benjamin says. "I'll deal with your 'not practicing' later, Petronia. Right now, there's someone at the door."

The door swings opens to Sunny, Boomer, Lars, Rasta, and all of Petronia's other friends! Boomer is holding his cello; Sunny has a harmonica; Rasta has his bass and even Lars brought his trombone!

"Petronia, are we too late to accompany you in the song we've been practicing?" asks Sunny.

"No, you're just in time!" Petronia shouts.

Sunny secretly hands Petronia the sheet music to
her song, while he distracts Benjamin with his
harmonica playing. This causes her dad to ask,
"What is all this, Petronia?"

"It's my special band, Dad! Are you guys ready?"
asks Petronia. "Of course, we're ready, we
practiced enough!" Sunny says, covering up for
Petronia.

Sunny, Lars, Rasta, and Boomer join Uncle Miles,
Max, and Izzy, so Petronia now has a great band to
help her play her song.

With her friends and family backing her, Petronia
sings, only this time, it sounds great!

Outside, people of all walks of life look up to see where the music is coming from. Thanks to her friends and family joining her, her song is a huge success.

It's important to have friends and family when you doubt yourself, especially when you haven't practiced like Petronia! You can always count on them!

Everyone is singing the lyrics to Petronia's new song:

"This time of year, it's important to know, that wishes and dreams are surrounded by love."

The singing grows louder and louder, and the lights grow brighter and brighter. The city has never seemed so united and at peace. Even the birds across the street sing along.

A confident Petronia continues to sing her song, realizing that her dream only came true because of the help from her friends and family.

Even though Benjamin is disappointed, he is overwhelmed with joy as he witnesses all the love and support his daughter has brought to their home with her new song, "This Time of Year."

Allegra, Petronia's mother, is equally proud. As she stands at Petronia's window in the next room, the beam of light shines brightly down on her.

Go to our website: www.asparrowstale.com
for more information.

Make sure you practice, continue to chase your dreams
and, most important, believe in yourself!

Until the next time, may all your "Wishettes" come true!

Please scan the QR code to hear Petronia's song:
"This Time of Year"